Father Christmas
on the Naughty Step

written by **Mark Sperring**

illustrated by **Tom McLaughlin**

PUFFIN

Today was
Christmas Eve
and Sam could have

been doing any number

of lovely things.

He could have been making something yummy
with his big sister Nellie . . .

or helping Rover with a last-minute letter to Santa . . .

Dear Santa,

The News

Naughty List Panic Sweeps the country Could you be on it this year?

or just day-dreaming with Dad about all the wonderful Christmassy things to come.

But Sam wasn't doing any of those lovely things . . .

Sam was sitting all by himself on the naughty step.
Until the naughty step gave a familiar

creeeaak...

And – **shiver me timbers!** –
    down sat someone who'd sat there
    a **zillion** times before.

"Have **you** been **naughty AGAIN?**" sighed Sam.

Captain Buckleboots gave a woeful nod.
    "Oh, Sam," he said. "I told the most
    terrible lie."

Then he held up a letter
for Sam to see.

Dear Santa,
Even though it might sound odd, my shipmates DEFINITELY do not want any Christmas presents this year. So can I please have theirs?
Many thanks,
Captain Buckleboots

"Oh dear," said Sam. "I can't imagine anything NAUGHTIER."

But just then, high above their heads, came the **jingle-jangle** of bells and a **flurry** of **snow**.

And – **shiver me tinsels!** –
down sat Father Christmas.

"SANTA!" gasped Sam. "It's Christmas Eve,
shouldn't you be getting ready to deliver
lots of lovely presents?"

Father Christmas gave a shameful sigh and
shuffled nervously on the naughty step.

"Yes," he said, "but I've been BAD
when I should have been GOOD!"

Then they saw it, dear oh dear . . .
Santa's name right at the TOP
of the **naughty list**.

"It all began this morning," explained Santa.

"I took something that clearly did NOT belong to me.

And even though I knew I SHOULDN'T, well . . .

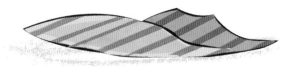

'STOP!' cried the elves as
I hurtled out of the workshop.

'STOP!' neighed the reindeer
as I sped down the hill.

But, blistering baubles,
I COULDN'T STOP!

CRASH!

BANG!

And suddenly everything was everywhere . . .

To make matters worse,

I started to LAUGH.

But, ho-ho-hum . . .
not everyone found it
quite so funny.

"Now," sighed Santa,
    "all I **really** want for Christmas
        is to be **forgiven**,
    but I don't know how."

For a moment, a sorrowful *hush*
fell over the naughty step.

    Then Sam had a
            wonderful **idea** . . .

"If you REALLY want to be forgiven," said Sam,
"you'll have to **show** you're really **sorry** . . .

then you'll have to
help the elves reload
the sleigh . . .

First you'll need to pick up all
the presents for the reindeer . . .

and, last but not least,
you must **promise**
NEVER to do it again."

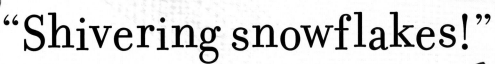

"Shivering snowflakes!"
said Father Christmas. "That's
exactly what I'll do!"

Just then, Sam's mum called out from the kitchen,
"You can get off the naughty step now!"

And off they all went to say a *heartfelt*
and very **seasonal** **sorry**.

"Sorry, me hearties,"
said Captain Buckleboots.

"Sorry," said Sam
oh so sweetly.

And the next morning . . .

not only did Sam find **lots**
of presents under the tree,
but also a most
surprising apology . . .

To Sam, I'm sorry I took your new train before you'd even had a chance to play with it. Next time I promise to ASK first. Have a merry christmas and BE GOOD, Love Santa xx

So, despite Christmas getting off to a
bit of a bad start, in the end a very . . .

Happy Christmas
was had by all.

For Mali J – Siôn Corn – M.S.

For Sarah, Eleanor, Amelia and Nathalia – T.M.

PUFFIN BOOKS
Published by the Penguin Group: London, New York,
Australia, Canada, India, Ireland, New Zealand and South Africa
Penguin Books Ltd, Registered Offices:
80 Strand, London WC2R 0RL, England
puffinbooks.com
First published 2012
Text copyright © Mark Sperring, 2012
Illustrations copyright © Tom McLaughlin, 2012
Made and printed in China
ISBN: 978–0–141–34306–8
002 – 10 9 8 7 6 5 4 3 2